FINDING GRACE

KIM SIGAFUS

7th GENERATION

Summertown, Tennessee

Library of Congress Cataloging-in-Publication Data
available upon request.

Cover and interior design: John Wincek

7th Generation
Book Publishing Company
PO Box 99, Summertown, TN 38483
888-260-8458
bookpubco.com
nativevoicesbooks.com

ISBN: 978-1-939053-29-9

25 24 23 22 21 20   1 2 3 4 5 6 7 8 9

Thank you to all my friends who have to deal with dyslexia on a day-to-day basis. To see where they started and how far they have come is truly an inspiration. It is my hope that Autumn Dawn's story will encourage those who struggle with a learning disability to keep pushing on. There is a light at the end of the tunnel, and it is worth it to make it there. Remember, it's the journey that teaches us, not the destination.

CONTENTS

The Dance

Standing on the sidelines of the large arena, Autumn clasped her hands in front of her and sighed. She was so nervous. To even be there was a huge deal for her. Normally she would prefer to sit in the audience and applaud those who were brave enough to put themselves out there and dance for hundreds of people. On top of that, this was a contest, so she was being judged. While Aunt Jessie clearly thought she was ready, she didn't feel ready.

This was an important time, for the Jingle Dress dance was one hundred years old now. Aunt Jessie had told her the dance had come about in Minnesota during the Spanish flu epidemic. The dance was a healing one, and the first dance was said to have healed a sick little girl. Every Jingle Dress dancer dances for others who are sick or hurting in some way. Autumn knew it to be a very powerful dance of prayer.

She watched as the music started and a young girl began dancing. She moved methodically and gracefully, and it was obvious to Autumn that the girl had been dancing all her life. The dance seemed to become a part of her, and Autumn wondered if her own dancing would give away how nervous she really was to even be there.

She glanced behind her to see Aunt Jessie smiling at her. Her father and mother were there as well, and Adam sat beside them in the bleachers with a grin on his face.

She smiled back at them as she adjusted the beaded necklace her father had made for her. Her red dress was simple, with sequins sewn into designs. She wore a white beaded belt and held a beautiful fan Aunt Jessie had given her. It had been hers when she danced many years ago, and Autumn felt honored to be gifted with it.

A minute later Autumn's number was called, and for a moment, she froze. Taking a deep breath, she closed her eyes for a minute and then took her place and waited for the music to begin.

When the drums began, Autumn started moving to their beat, picturing herself as a graceful butterfly. The three hundred and sixty-five jingles moved in rhythm as she danced around her space in the arena. Her traditional steps were bouncy, and as she moved, she sent prayers out to those people who were suffering in some way. She knew some people were dealing with terminal illnesses or death, and some even had missing daughters. Reservations were known for having missing women that no one in the outside world seemed to care about. Autumn could feel the sorrow those families felt, and as she made a half-turn, she glanced up at her family sitting in the bleachers. She danced for them as well, hoping the healing prayers she was sending out would help repair the damage that her family had done to themselves.

As soon as it had begun, it was over. There was applause as Autumn walked to the sidelines of the arena, breathing heavily. Her red dress glittered in the arena lights, and she pulled her two braids in front of her, trying to cool off her neck. The girl next to her gave her a smile, and she suddenly realized that she was now part of a very special group of people. She was a Jingle Dress dancer.

When the whole group was finished, they all walked off the sidelines and headed for their families. Autumn walked over to hers, and Aunt Jessie reached out to hug her excitedly, telling her how wonderful she did.

"I am so proud of you," said her father, giving her a smile over Jessie's head. "That was just beautiful."

He had his arm around her mother, and Autumn turned to smile at her, watching her tear up.

"You looked so grown-up out there," she whispered. "I did a double take when I saw you. I almost didn't recognize you."

Autumn smiled and turned away, embarrassed by her mother's tearful emotions.

"Miika."

Adam had taken a step toward her and raised her chin with his fingers. "I have never seen anything like that," he said softly. "It was so graceful."

She smiled, and a warm look filled her eyes.

"Thank you," she said, taking his hand and giving it a squeeze. He reached over to kiss her cheek.

They helped her get settled and then waited for the contest results. It wasn't long before they were announced. Autumn didn't place, but it didn't matter to her. In her mind, she had won first place for even going out there. She was proud of herself.

The drive back to Aunt Jessie's apartment was a good one. Autumn's parents drove Jessie's SUV, and Jessie was in the middle seat talking with them. Adam and Autumn were sitting in the last row of seats, holding hands and whispering back and forth. Every once in a while Autumn's dad, Tom, would glance back at them, and Autumn would give him a smile and nod. She knew he was watching them, but it didn't matter. Adam was very respectful of her family.

Jessie was talking excitedly about the pow wow and noted that every once in a while Autumn's mother, Melissa, would reach up to touch the gorgeous beaded necklace Tom had made for her. It matched Autumn's in design, but he had used all her favorite colors while making it.

Jessie wondered how things were going with the two of them. From the outside things looked great, but she knew her brother had a temper and wondered how that figured into things.

Melissa looked happy. Jessie knew she was proud of her daughter, but as she caught the smile Melissa was giving her brother, she hoped Tom was working hard to make Melissa happy as well.

"Aunt Jessie?"

Jessie turned now to see Autumn leaning forward in the seat.

"Yes?"

"How's Ryan?"

She turned back around. "He's fine."

"Just fine?"

"Yup."

"That's it? That's all you're going to say?"

"Yup."

"Come on . . . fess up. What's going on with you two? Is he still asking you to marry him all the time? Did you ever grow a brain and finally accept?"

"Autumn Dawn, that's no way to talk to your aunt," scolded her mother.

"Ryan asked you to marry him?" Tom shook his head. "You haven't known him that long, Jessie. No wonder you turned him down."

"Who said I turned him down?"

Autumn squealed, and Melissa laughed at Tom's shocked expression. She leaned over the seat to give Jessie's hand a squeeze.

"I am so happy for you!" she said with a smile.

Jessie grinned as Autumn's hug strangled her from behind.

"When is the wedding?" asked Autumn. "Can I be in it? Is it going to be in Minneapolis or are you going to come back to the rez? You still have a lot of friends there, you know. Maybe Sam can be the ring bearer. What colors are you going with? Wait . . . it's going to be a big wedding, right? You aren't just going to the courthouse and getting married by a judge, because . . . "

"Hold on a minute," interrupted Jessie with a laugh. "Settle down and breathe for a moment so I can answer some of your questions."

"Congrats, Jessie," said Adam. "I hope you will be very happy."

"Thank you. And can I say how happy I am you and Autumn have found each other?" she replied. "It makes me happy to see her so happy."

He smiled at her and then glanced at Autumn, who was blushing. He laughed.

"I guess you found a way to stop her from talking," he noted, and everyone laughed.

"Jessie, are you sure about this?" asked Tom, frowning from the driver's side of the car. "You haven't known him that long."

"I have known him for several years, Tom. He drives me nuts, but I suspect any man would." She paused a moment and then caught Tom's eyes in the rearview mirror. "I love him," she added quietly, and after a moment, Tom nodded.

"Then I am happy for you, sis. You deserve happiness."

"Thank you."

Tom sighed, and Melissa reached out for his hand as Jessie started to tell everyone the details.

"Minawaanigotaagozi," she said quietly, and he nodded.

"Yes, I know she is happy," he replied. He turned to glance at her a moment. "Hey, you just spoke Ojibwa."

She nodded. "I'm trying to learn some of the language . . . for us," she added, and he nodded.

"Thank you. It's a good start." He paused and then added, "I hope someday I can say those words regarding you, Melissa. You have been unhappy too long."

"I know. But I am hoping that will all change."

"Me, too. I will do my best to make it so."

"Mom," interrupted Autumn, "Aunt Jessie just said that she will be having a big wedding in Minneapolis. Can we go?"

"Of course," replied Melissa, turning around to face her. "We wouldn't miss that for the world."

"Melissa, would you be my matron of honor?" asked Jessie.

"Me? Oh . . . I . . . of course. I mean, yes!"

Jessie laughed. "I do think Sam would be cute as my ring bearer. It is going to be a wedding with traditional Native aspects. I would like him to wear a traditional Native outfit of some kind. We can talk about it later when I start to really plan."

"When is the wedding?" asked Tom. "Have you picked a date yet?"

"The third Saturday in May. We're heading out on a honeymoon the day after."

"Where are you going?"

"Ryan won't tell me. He said somewhere warm, though."

"It sounds so romantic," said Autumn, leaning her chin on the back of Jessie's seat.

"You know, the wedding is only eight months away," pointed out Melissa. "It sometimes takes six to eight months for dresses to come into the dress shop."

"That's true," replied Jessie. "Hmm . . . maybe we should go looking tomorrow before you go home. My friend Barb is the manager of the bridal shop in Lake of the Isles. I'll call her and see if she can fit us in sometime tomorrow. Maybe she can open the shop up early for me if she is booked, or maybe we can come in after it is officially closed."

Jessie picked up her cell phone and punched in some numbers. Barb answered, and they talked for a few moments before Jessie hung up.

"She opens up at ten in the morning," she said. "But she is willing to open up two hours early so we can go through the store and see if we can find anything we would like to try on."

"So, that would be eight, right?"

"Yes. I know it's early, but she is doing us a favor . . ."

"When are we leaving for home, Tom?" asked Melissa. "Will that work with your schedule?"

That was the first time she had ever tried to work with his schedule, and he was grateful for that.

"I don't work tomorrow, so we can leave whenever we want to," he said.

"Tom, would you walk me down the aisle and give me away?"

Tom's intake of breath was audible, and he choked up a little as he caught Jessie's gaze in the rearview mirror.

He nodded as he cleared his throat. "Of course. I would be honored."

"Can we all come and watch you try on dresses?" asked Autumn, leaning back in her seat now.

"Well, yes, but I was hoping you would try on a few as well," answered Jessie. "After all, you are my bridesmaid."

Autumn squealed again, and Adam laughed as she hugged him and then leaned over the seat to hug Jessie.

Melissa and Tom laughed as Autumn let go of her aunt and settled back in her seat.

"I want to thank you guys for being an inspiration for me," Jessie said, addressing Melissa and Tom. She pushed her hair behind her ear and gave them a smile.

"Us?" asked Melissa. "What did we do?"

"Your relationship is inspiring."

"It is? But we are divorced."

"Yes, but you both see the mistakes you made in the marriage and are trying to fix them. I can see how much you love each other."

Tom nodded. "I know I am trying to be a better man, and I can see Melissa is trying as well to make things work."

"That inspires me. Watching you two has taught me that relationships don't have to be perfect to work. In some ways, Ryan is the complete opposite of me. But we have the same core values, and he will make a good husband for me."

"He is lucky to have you," said Melissa, and Jessie smiled.

"Thank you."

As the women settled back in their seats, Tom watched Autumn slip her hand out of Adam's. As she looked away and stared out the window, Tom wondered what his daughter was thinking.

Adam glanced at her and sighed, meeting Tom's gaze in the rearview mirror. He shrugged and looked away, and Tom turned his attention back to the road.

A Crisis Arises

B re and Jayden watched as Adam led Autumn into the school. They were an "item" now, as they joined the ranks of the other couples in the school.

It was a weird feeling for Autumn, who was used to being alone and friendless. She still didn't have any friends, but Adam told her she was his best friend, and she wanted to see him that way, too. Her feelings about him were very confusing. She liked him but was afraid of getting hurt, which made her pull away now and then. Adam noticed when she did this, and she could see how much it hurt him. He said nothing, because he knew she was dealing with her demons regarding relationships. He just hoped she'd get things straightened out in her own mind and not kick him out of her life again.

Bre and Jayden glared at Autumn as the couple headed for their lockers. Even though their lockers were not near each other, Adam opened Autumn's and then helped her get things put away. They both had a big project due that week, and they were carrying stuff back and forth from school to home and back to school again.

"Thanks," said Autumn, shutting the locker door and transferring her books to her left arm. Adam smiled again and took her right hand as they headed for his locker.

"Can you believe it?" whispered Bre. "That girl has managed to get her hooks in Adam. He could've had his pick of any girl in school and he picked her!"

"I know. There must be a reason he hangs around with her," replied Jayden. "She's not that cute. As a matter of fact, I think she's fat."

The girls giggled as Sydney walked up to them. She was carrying her project, too, and was trying to balance it in her arms along with her books.

"What are you two idiots laughing about now?"

They looked up to see Sydney glaring at them.

"Autumn, of course," replied Bre. "And who are you calling idiots?"

"I call them like I see them," answered Sydney, starting to walk down the hall again.

"Wait! Sydney!"

The girls ran down the hall after their friend and began walking beside her.

"Where have you been?" asked Bre. "I've been calling your house every day. Your mom says you're busy. You can't be that busy. Why don't you ever call me back?"

"I am busy," stated Sydney, not looking at Bre. "What did you want?"

"Jayden and I were going shopping. We wanted you to come with us."

"Yeah," said Jayden. "Mom gave me money to get some new shoes. I was going to look for a pair with two-inch heels."

"You'd fall and break your neck in those," replied Sydney. "Why would you ever buy a pair of shoes like that?"

"You said they were classy, remember? The last time we went shopping, you said, 'Those are some classy-lookin' shoes.'" Jayden stared at Sydney now. "What's the matter with you anyway? You never hang out with us anymore, and you never take our calls."

"Nothing's the matter," Sydney answered. "I'm just busy."

"Too busy for your friends?" asked Bre.

Sydney stopped by her locker and fiddled with the lock.

"Look, I have a lot going on right now at home. Dad's moved out and Mom's mad all the time." She pulled open her locker and shoved her stuff in it, slamming it shut. "And now I have to take this stupid tutoring class after school."

"Isn't Autumn in that class?"

"Yes. So?"

"So, it gives you the chance to torment her some more."

Sydney turned to stare at Bre. "I have better things to do than torment Autumn. Besides, she has Adam backing her up now."

"Yeah, we can't figure that out. A chubby girl like that shouldn't be able to get a guy like him."

"Chubby? Really, Bre?" Sydney shook her head. "Why don't you grow up? Adam's with her because he likes her. End of story." Sydney turned and started to walk away. "I suggest you guys find something better to do with your time," she added. "Leave Autumn alone."

The girls watched Sydney disappear around the corner and then turned to look at each other.

"What the heck just happened?" asked Jayden.

"She's defending Autumn. She's been tormenting the girl for years and now she's defending her." Bre thought for a moment and then added, "Maybe Autumn has something on her."

"What do you mean?"

"Well, maybe Autumn knows something and is holding it over Sydney's head."

"Like what?"

"I don't know. But it's not like Sydney to just stop giving Autumn a hard time. Something must have happened."

"I guess." Jayden looked up to note they were the only ones in the hall. "Let's go," she said. "We're going to be late."

Autumn glanced up as Bre entered the room. The bell rang as she slid into her seat and glanced over at Autumn. Autumn looked away and concentrated on the teacher.

I wonder if she does have something on Sydney, thought Bre, finally looking away to concentrate on the paper the teacher was handing out. A smile crossed her face as a thought came to her.

Adam can't be with her all the time. She would corner Autumn when she could get her by herself and demand to know what was going on. After all, she was Sydney's best friend and she would stick up for her.

As Bre took the paper from the teacher, Autumn caught her smile. Autumn had known her a long time, and she was obviously up to no good. It probably had something to do with her.

Autumn slumped in her seat and sighed. With Sydney outright ignoring her now, she thought maybe she was in the clear. But it looked like Bre had other ideas. And no doubt, Jayden wasn't far behind.

Lunchtime came around, and Autumn was sitting at a table trying to decide if she was going to eat the school's definition of pizza. She had eaten everything else on her tray and was contemplating dumping it when Adam entered the cafeteria.

She went to give him a smile, but all of a sudden Bre sat down across from her.

"I want to talk to you," she said, and Autumn grimaced.

"What about?" Autumn asked, watching Adam look in her direction. She and Adam didn't have the same lunchtime, so she was surprised to see him. He walked over to the lunchroom supervisor with a note, and after a short conversation and a nod from the supervisor, Adam headed Autumn's way.

Bree tapped Autumn's hand to get her attention. "Listen, dummy. I'm trying to talk to you."

"You're done talking to her like that," stated Adam, coming up behind Bre. She turned to look at him, and he stuck his thumb out to indicate she should move.

"We're in the middle of something," said Bre, ignoring him as she turned back around to glare at Autumn.

"No one is interested in hearing it," he stated. "Come on, Autumn."

He took her tray, and Autumn stood up and followed him to the garbage can to dump it.

"Adam?"

"How long has she been there bothering you?"

"Not long. Ah . . . why are you here? This isn't your lunch period."

"I handed in some paperwork to the office a few minutes ago and was in there when the call came in."

"Call?"

"Yeah."

When he said nothing further, she turned and caught his gaze.

"Okay, you're scaring me. What's going on?"

"There's been an accident."

"Accident? What do you mean? Who? What happened?"

Fear clutched Autumn's heart as Adam explained that her mother and Sam had been hit by a car while crossing the street uptown.

"I have to go. Where's Dad? What hospital are they in? How am I going to get there?"

"They are in Mahnomen Health Center. Your father is on his way to pick you up. They sent me to tell you because they know we are close, and they are dealing with another emergency in the office." He shrugged. "Usually, it's the adults who are supposed to handle this sort of thing. With the emergency happening, I don't think they had a choice but to send me to get you and bring you to the office." He took her hand. "Okay, let's head to your locker and grab your stuff."

Autumn dropped his hand and ran down the hall to her locker and tried to get it open.

"I hate this lock," she muttered when Adam caught up with her and pushed her hands away to do it for her.

"What was the emergency in the office?" she asked, glancing down the hallway.

"Will had a seizure, I think."

"Oh no. Is he going to be okay?"

"They called the ambulance."

"Not a good day."

"Nope."

The bell rang as they ran down the hall toward the office. Kids were pushing and shoving their way down the hall trying to get to class or the next lunch period. Adam took Autumn's hand again and managed to get her to the office door.

The principal spotted her in the doorway.

"Your father is out front," she said, and Autumn nodded. Adam followed her out the door of the school.

"Wait," Autumn said, grabbing his arm. "Are you supposed to leave the school?"

He nodded. "My aunt is subbing for the nurse today. I told her I was leaving with you."

"That was okay?"

He grinned. "Probably not. But she will call my nokomis and let her know."

"Your grandmother will be alright with it?"

"I hope so."

Tom's truck was right outside the door. They jumped into it, and Tom quickly pulled out of the parking lot.

"Dad, have you seen them?" asked Autumn, shoving her book bag on the floor.

He shook his head, pushing his long black hair out of his face. He glanced at her, and she could see the fear in his eyes.

She reached out her hand to take his. He nodded and then glanced at Adam, who had hold of her other hand.

Adam wondered for a moment if Tom would pull over and make him get out of the truck. After all, this was a family matter.

Tom glanced from Autumn's face to Adam's. He nodded and turned away as they made their way to Mahnomen.

CHAPTER 3

Talking It Out

Sam was lying very still in the hospital bed. His head was facing away from them, and his eyes were closed when they walked in. Autumn's mother, Melissa, was in surgery.

Autumn teared up as she stopped just inside the door. Adam pulled her closer as Tom stepped into the room and walked over to his son's bed.

Sam slowly opened his eyes and turned his head. His eyes lit up as he saw his father, and his bottom lip started to quiver.

Just then, the nurse came in. Tom ignored her as he comforted his son, sitting on the bed and letting Sam sit up slowly before he carefully pulled him into his arms.

"He was lucky," the nurse stated, glancing at them. "When Melissa was hit, she somehow had the presence of mind to turn her body to shield Sam from hitting the sidewalk. He landed on her as they fell. He's scraped up a little, but he'll be fine."

The nurse shook her head. "Two people saw it happen. They had to pry him from her arms as she lay there unconscious."

"That's my woman," murmured Tom, closing his eyes as he hugged Sam, who was nestling into his arms.

"Is Sam alright?" asked Autumn, pulling away from Adam.

"Like I said, he's a little banged up," replied the nurse. "But I think the doctor will release him later today or tomorrow morning. They just want to keep an eye on him for a while in case anything crops up." She smiled. "We put him in a regular child's bed. It's lower to the floor. He climbed right out of the crib we had in here."

Autumn smiled at that. "I see," she said, glancing over at her father. "What do we do now?"

"I told the doctor who is working on Mom where we are going to be. When they are done with surgery, I will be called," Tom replied.

"So we'll stay in here then?" asked Autumn.

"For now." Tom glanced over at the nurse. "That's alright, isn't it?"

The nurse nodded. "Of course." She turned and started to walk out of the room but stopped at the doorway and turned around. Her eyes grew soft. "I'm sorry about the accident," she said quietly. "But I'm glad your little guy is alright. Hopefully things will go well for your wife."

After the nurse left, Autumn went to sit down on the bed, and Adam walked over to the blue chair in the corner and sat down. Tom got up as Sam crawled into his sister's arms.

"I'm going to get some coffee," he said in a tired voice. "I think it's going to be a while until we hear about Mom."

Autumn nodded as she watched him leave. Then she looked over at Adam.

"What if Mom doesn't pull through?" she whispered, but he caught it and got up to sit next to her on the bed. She laid her head on his shoulder, trying to hold back the tears. Her father had asked her not to cry in front of Sam, as it might scare him.

"Where's Mama?" asked Sam.

"She's with the doctor right now," Autumn replied, feeling a tear slide down her cheek. She cleared her throat.

"Don't cry," Sam said, clumsily wiping the tear away with his fingers. "I'm okay."

She smiled and hugged him tight.

"I am so glad about that," she said.

"Me, too," said Adam.

The nurse entered again, but this time she brought a box of toys with her.

"We keep this box for the special kids that come in here," she said, setting it down on the bed. Sam scrambled over to it and started digging toys out. When he found the little cars, he squealed.

"Thank you," said Autumn, and the nurse nodded and left the room.

"Are you hungry?" asked Adam. "I could go down and get you some food from the cafeteria."

She shrugged. "I don't know. I'm feeling kind of . . . well . . . I don't know."

Adam nodded, understanding. "I'll go get you a drink. I'll be right back."

Autumn nodded gratefully and he left.

Walking down the long hall, he wondered if he should call his mom or grandmother. He wanted to make sure they knew that he had left school and where he had gone.

He pulled his phone out as he headed for the cafeteria. On the way, he passed the chapel and paused, as he saw Tom sitting in a pew with a cup of coffee in his hand.

Without even thinking about it, Adam shoved the phone back into his pocket and opened the door quietly to walk in. He went to the pew Tom was in and sat down next to him. Tom glanced over in surprise and took a drink of coffee, watching him.

"Are you religious?" asked Adam.

Tom shrugged. "Under the circumstances, praying can't hurt."

"True," Adam said, smiling a little.

"Why are you here, Adam?"

"What do you mean?"

"Why are you here at the hospital with us? Surely you are missing school."

"I want to be here for Autumn."

"Why?"

"I'm her friend."

Tom grinned in spite of himself. "Friend?"

"Friend," replied Adam firmly. When he caught Tom's skeptical gaze, he looked away and shrugged. "I care about her."

"I can see that. But how far has this friendship gone?"

"We hold hands, and I've kissed her," replied Adam, uncomfortably. "But no more."

"There will be no more."

Adam nodded. "Of course you're going to say that."

"I mean it."

"I'm aware of the way you feel about me."

"That has nothing to do with it."

Adam glanced at him. "I would never hurt her."

"But she has hurt you?"

"Yes." Adam glanced over at him. "How did you know that?"

"I have eyes and ears." Tom shook his head then. "Yet you do not leave her."

"No."

Tom took another drink of his coffee and sighed.

"Why are you in the chapel?" he asked.

"I saw you in here," answered Adam.

"So?"

"So I thought you could use some company."

Tom turned to stare at him for a moment, and then he took another drink, still watching Adam.

"Your Native name is 'Makoons'?"

Adam nodded. "Does Sam have an Ojibwa name?"

Tom shook his head. "Melissa didn't think it was important." Seeing Adam's look, he added, "We weren't in the best place when he was born. We didn't agree on anything at that point. I left shortly after."

Tom took one last drink of his coffee, finishing it up.

"Let's go back," he said, getting up.

"I promised Autumn a sandwich and drink," replied Adam.

"I'll get it," said Tom, walking over to the chapel door and pulling it open.

Adam nodded as they walked through the door, letting it shut quietly behind them. Just then, the intercom popped on.

"Code blue, fifth floor. Code blue, fifth floor."

Tom and Adam started walking down the hall toward the cafeteria.

"How long did you say Melissa will be in surgery?" asked Adam.

"They said five or six hours."

"Wow, that's a long time."

They moved to the right side of the hall when two people ran by.

"Must be responding to the code blue," remarked Adam.

"Yeah," said Tom.

"So should Autumn and I go up to the surgical floor in case they look for us there?" asked Adam as they entered the cafeteria.

"Well, they said they would get ahold of us when surgery was over, and I told them where we were going. There is a waiting room on the fifth floor. I suppose you two could . . ."

Just then, Adam's phone began to ring.

"Shoot . . . I'm sorry. I forgot to shut that off," he said with a grimace.

He pulled the phone out of his pocket and glanced at it.

"It's Autumn," he said, frowning.

"Fifth floor is where surgical is . . ." muttered Tom, thinking about the code blue announcement. Pushing his hand through his hair, he started to speak his thoughts quickly in Ojibwa.

Adam answered the phone with a frown.

"Hi, Autumn. What?" Adam glanced over at Tom. "She's been trying to reach you."

"What? Why?" Tom pulled out his phone and looked down at it. "I turned it off when we entered the hospital, and . . . oh no, I turned it off." He looked over at Adam, who was nodding.

"We're on our way," said Adam, and he pushed the button to end the call. He shoved the phone in his pocket, grabbed Tom's arm, and started dragging him down the hall.

"That code blue was Melissa," Adam said with a grim look on his face. "They need us in the surgical waiting room right now."

"Autumn . . ."

"She's already there," Adam said. "She left Sam with a nurse."

They took the stairs rather than the elevator to save time. They burst into the surgical waiting room to see Autumn talking with a nurse. She was sobbing, and the nurse was trying to console her.

"What's going on?" asked Tom, grabbing the nurse by the arm. "Is Melissa . . . ?"

The nurse shook her head. "Your wife stopped breathing during the operation," she said quietly. "They are trying to resuscitate her. I'm sorry, but that's all I know."

Tom looked over to see that Adam had moved Autumn to a chair and was sitting down with her on his lap. He was holding her close as she sobbed.

"How did this happen?" Tom whispered, addressing the nurse. "I didn't think she was that bad."

"Sir, your wife had internal injuries," the nurse replied. "She was bleeding inside. They had to go in and try to stop that."

"I . . . I . . ." Tom turned away. "I guess I didn't know what that meant." He pushed back a sob. "What do we do now?"

"You wait," answered the nurse quietly. "Someone will be out to talk to you shortly."

He watched the nurse walk away and then stood there for several minutes, not moving. He glanced over at Adam and Autumn and then at the door, thinking about Sam.

Slowly, he took his phone out of his pocket and pushed a button. It started to dial.

After a moment, a soft voice picked up, and he couldn't hold back the sobs any longer.

"Jessie? It's me. Melissa is . . . I need you to come right away." He took a breath and added, "I think she's going to die."

"What? What happened?"

"There was an accident . . ."

"I'm on my way," replied Jessie. "The hospital in Mahnomen?"

"Yes."

"I'll call you along the way."

"Okay," whispered Tom as he hung up.

Seeing the pain in his eyes, Autumn got up and walked over to him. She knew they were echoing what was in hers as well.

There were three other people in the waiting room with them, and they had been watching and listening. One by one, they all got up and went to the little family standing in the middle of the surgical waiting room floor. They put their arms around them and started to pray.

Adam stood outside the circle for a moment, watching. Then he joined the group, and in the stillness of the room, and for the first time in his life, he started to pray.

CHAPTER

4

The Surprise Visitor

The three of them stood around Melissa's hospital bed. She had a tube in her nose helping her to breathe, and she was lying very still. Her face was pale and drawn.

The doctor had told them that even though they had been able to revive her, she had been without oxygen for a long time. It wasn't clear to anyone if she would actually make it or not.

Sam was napping. He complained that his arm hurt, so the doctor gave him something to help him rest for a while.

Jessie had called back and was due to arrive at any minute. She had left right after talking to Tom. Ryan was also coming up that night after work.

Tom approached the bed and sat down in a chair next to it. He pushed Melissa's hair out of her face and leaned in to whisper to her.

"Melissa? Can you hear me?" He took her hand in his and added, "I'm here."

There was no response, and Melissa didn't move. Autumn choked back a sob, and Adam pulled her closer.

For some reason, he felt like he belonged there in that room with Melissa's family. Even though he and Autumn had been seeing each other for such a short time, he knew he was needed. She could lean on him, and he would see to it that the family had what they needed to get through this terrible time.

Tom glanced up to see his daughter crying softly and being cradled in Adam's shoulder. He had his arm protectively around her and was rubbing her back. He caught Tom's gaze and looked back at him with intelligence and knowledge well beyond his years. He looked like a young man who had gone through some hard times himself and made it through.

Tom sighed, not liking how close Adam and Autumn were getting but understanding that this was not the time to have that conversation. He was slightly irritated to discover that he liked the young man. He didn't want to, but there wasn't much to dislike.

The nurse walked in and took Melissa's vitals, and Tom got up and moved away for a moment. He went over to the hospital room window and peered out, seeing nothing. The rain had started, and he could hear the patter of drops hitting the roof below the window.

"There has been no change."

Tom turned to see the nurse addressing him from the bed. She was straightening the covers over Melissa.

"The surgery . . . how did that go?"

The nurse looked at Tom in surprise. "Didn't the doctor go over all that with you?"

Tom nodded and glanced away. "Yes, but I didn't understand what he was talking about."

The nurse took Melissa's chart and walked over to Tom.

"Well, she was thrown when the car hit her," she began, and Tom nodded.

"She hit her head on the pavement and was pretty scraped up," Tom said.

"Yes," said the nurse. "She also has internal injuries, and that's what the surgery was for."

"What were they?"

"The accident damaged her spleen, splitting it open. This caused blood to flood into the abdominal cavity. There was also damage to the liver. It was torn open."

"Did the surgery work?" Tom asked.

"They repaired everything," the nurse replied.

"Then why did she stop breathing?"

"She landed on her head. She suffered a small stroke and had brain swelling." The nurse glanced over at Melissa. "She's lucky to be alive. The car was going fast and hit her hard."

She sighed. "This has all been so hard for her little body to take. You have to give her some time to heal."

"So, she will heal then?" Tom said.

"All we can do is pray." The nurse hesitated and then added, "There's a chapel in this hospital. Have you been there? Some people like to pray in a church-like setting."

"Gitchie Manitou hears prayers anywhere," Tom replied. "I'm not leaving her."

The nurse nodded. "Alright then. There's a waiting room down the hall to your right. It has coffee and vending machines in it. If I can do anything more for you, let me know."

The nurse left, and Autumn went to stand by her dad, who put his arm around her. He kissed the top of her forehead and sighed.

"I guess we just wait," he said, and she nodded.

"I hate waiting," she said, and he smiled faintly.

"Me, too."

"Can I get either of you anything?"

They turned to look at Adam. He shoved his hands into his front pockets and shrugged.

"If you're hungry or thirsty, I can go down to the cafeteria and get you something."

"Go get Autumn something," instructed Tom, reaching into his wallet and handing the boy some money. "Bring back something for yourself."

"Dad, you need something, too," said Autumn, pulling another five out of his wallet.

"Get Dad and me the same thing," she said, handing the money to Adam, who nodded. He turned and left the room.

Tom watched him leave, and Autumn smiled.

"You like him, don't you, Dad?"

He looked down at her and shook his head. "He's alright."

"He's a good guy," Autumn said.

"I guess."

Autumn smiled. "You don't want to like him, do you?"

"Not really. He's trying to take my little girl away from me."

"No, he's not. He just . . . well . . . likes me."

"I see the way he looks at you."

"Dad . . ."

"No. You see it, too, don't you? It scares you, and that's why you pull away."

Autumn shifted uncomfortably under his gaze.

"He hasn't tried anything, has he?"

"Dad . . ."

"No, I mean it. Has he tried anything?"

"Well, he kissed me and that's all."

"Really?"

"Really."

"Good. You're too young for anything more."

Autumn pulled back a little. "I'm growing up, you know. I'm not your little girl anymore."

"You'll always be my little girl."

"You know what I mean."

"Yes, I do. But you'd better be careful, young lady. Don't make me get my bow and arrows out and chase him all over town."

Autumn giggled and shook her head. "I won't," she promised, and Tom smiled down at her and relaxed a moment. Then he glanced over at the hospital bed Melissa was lying in.

"I think they are going to release Sam tonight or tomorrow morning," he said. "You may need to go home with him."

"What about Aunt Jessie? Isn't she coming?"

He nodded. "I think we will all have to take turns going home and watching him. We can take a shower and eat there, too." He looked at his watch. "I promised I'd call work back. They are waiting to hear when I will be back in."

He glanced over at Melissa. "I don't want to leave her, but I'm going to step out of the room for a moment."

Autumn nodded and watched him go. Then she went over and sat down on the bed next to her mother. She picked up the arm without the IV in it and laid it over herself. She lay down on the bed and snuggled next to her mother, closing her eyes.

"Mama," she whispered. "I don't know if you can hear me. I miss you. Please come back. Daddy needs you, and Sam does, too."

She closed her eyes and prayed, falling into an exhausted sleep moments later.

It was there Adam and Tom found her. After talking to his boss, Tom had been given the week off. He nodded as Adam handed him a sandwich and some coffee. He put a finger to his lips and motioned Adam out of the room.

"I think Autumn's asleep," he said, taking a sip of the hot brew. "I guess it's alright to go into the waiting room for a while and leave them be."

Adam took one last look at Autumn and then nodded.

"Alright."

As they entered the waiting room, they noticed a young man sitting in a chair under the window. He appeared to be in his late teens and was scrawny-looking with mousy brown hair. Neither Tom nor Adam recognized him, so they ignored him and looked for somewhere to sit. The man just stared at the floor and didn't acknowledge them.

Adam sat down on a long, padded bench and took a sip of his pop. Tom sat down by the door. For several minutes no one spoke.

"I'm sorry," the young man muttered to himself. "I didn't see her." He shook his head miserably. "It all happened so fast."

Tom looked up sharply and stared at him.

"What? Are you talking to me?"

The young man looked up. "I can't believe I hit someone. A woman with a baby." He looked down at the floor again. "I came here to see if she…" —he swallowed hard—"was alright. My mom works here as a nurse. She is so upset. She said the woman was probably up here . . . in surgical. If she's still . . ." He shook his head. "My mom made me come here."

"You didn't see her? Are you talking about my wife? Are you the one who hit my wife?"

"I . . . I don't know."

Tom jumped out of his seat and strode over to him.

"My wife was hit while crossing the street today. You hit her, didn't you? How could you not see her? She was in the crosswalk with a baby in her arms!"

"I . . . I was reaching down to change the radio station, and when I looked up again, I saw her," the young man whispered. "But it was too late. I hit her."

He saw the fury in Tom's gaze. He shuddered at the anger he could feel coming from him.

"Why are you here?" asked Adam.

The young man turned to look at him with watery eyes.

"I feel bad. I wanted to see what I could do."

"You have done . . ."

"Tom, no," said Adam quietly, and Tom swallowed down his retort reluctantly. He didn't know what it was about Adam, but he seemed to have a calming effect on those around him.

The young man stood up and shoved his hands into the pockets of his jeans.

"I shouldn't have come here," he said, clearing his throat.

"I'm glad you did."

The three men turned to see Jessie at the door. She had arrived in time to hear most of the conversation. She stepped through the door and reached out for Tom, who gratefully went into her arms to be held.

She smiled over at Adam, who nodded back at her, and then turned to look at the young man standing next to the window.

"I think you need to stay," she said, pulling out of Tom's arms. "We're all going to have to see this through together."

"Jessie, I don't think he should be here," replied Tom angrily. "He hit her! He's the reason she's in the hospital."

"Yup, and he needs to see what he's done. Life lessons can come from any place."

"I really think I should go . . . ," said the young man, but the doctor walking in interrupted him.

He looked around the room. "I was told I could find Melissa's family in here," he stated gruffly, and Tom nodded.

"Yes, we are it." He glanced at the young man over by the window and his eyes narrowed. He went to speak, but Jessie's hand on his arm stopped him.

"Yes, doctor?" she asked.

The doctor turned to look at her and nodded.

"There seems to be no change in Melissa's condition," he said, glancing at his notes. "She lost some blood and coded while on the table. We have her stabilized, but it took us a while to get her back." He looked up from his chart. "I wish I had better news for you, but right now all we can do is wait and see."

"How long?" asked Tom.

"As long as it takes," he replied. He sighed and dropped his hand with the chart in it. "Or until you have to make the decision to let her go."

"Let her go?"

The doctor took off his glasses and wiped them on his shirt. "I believe in telling families the truth. If she doesn't come out of the coma, you will have to decide whether to keep her alive on a ventilator or let her go. Even if she does come back, there is no guarantee what condition she will be in."

"There's nothing we can do?" asked Adam.

"Pray. It can't hurt."

"Yeah, I know," replied Tom.

The doctor turned to go and then turned back around in the doorway.

"Did you know she has AB negative blood? Very rare. If any one of you has that, we could use some, just in case."

"I do." Everyone turned to look at the young man under the window.

"I have AB negative blood," he said again. "I'll donate. I'll do it now."

"Good," said the doctor. With a nod to the others, he ushered the young man out of the room.

"Gitchie Manitou works in mysterious ways," murmured Jessie.

"What do you mean?" asked Tom.

"You wondered why that young man was here. I mean, who would hit someone and then come to the hospital to see if they were okay?"

"That's what I wondered."

"The kind of young man who has a conscience," she replied. "The kind of young man who is sorry."

"Oh, I don't know about that," muttered Tom.

"He just left to give blood to your wife," Adam pointed out.

"Without him, we wouldn't have it," said Jessie.

"Without him, we wouldn't need it," Tom countered.

"I wonder if there's more to the story than he's telling us," said Jessie. "Did Melissa look both ways before crossing the street? Did she step out in front of the car and he couldn't get around her?"

"He said he wasn't paying attention. He was fiddling with his radio. My wife is lying in a hospital bed because that kid hit her in the process of trying to find some rock station!" Tom shouted, shoving his hand into his long hair and pushing it off his face.

"Let's talk about her medical power of attorney."

"What?"

Jessie sighed. "Her power of attorney. You know, the one who makes decisions for her care."

Tom stared at her. "I'm her husband. I will have the final say."

"You are her ex-husband," Jessie pointed out. "You do not have the final say."

"Well, then, who does?"

"I do."

"You?" Tom looked at Jessie with disbelief.

"Yes. Melissa asked me a long time ago."

"So now you're telling me I don't even have any rights when it comes to her care?"

"You are the one who left, Tom," Jessie pointed out.

Tom stared at her a moment, and then, with a clenched jaw, he strode out of the waiting room door. The door slammed behind him.

CHAPTER 5

Unforgiven

I t was two in the morning, and Jessie woke Autumn to take her turn by her mother's bedside. She sat down next to her mother's bed and picked up her hand.

The silence gave Autumn plenty of time to think about what was going on around her. Sam had gone home, and her father had gone with him. The doctor thought it would be best for the little boy to have at least one of his parents there the first night when he went to bed, since he had just been released from the hospital.

Jessie was in the waiting room, sleeping. She had spent several hours with Melissa and, later, Tom, who had helped Sam get ready to leave the hospital. She had signed paperwork for Sam's release, and then turned the rest over to Tom. He had said very little, but she could tell he was fuming over the situation with the medical power of attorney.

She missed Ryan, but she had told him not to come. She wasn't sure what was going to happen now, and she felt he needed to be at work. There was nothing he could do here. He had objected, but she was firm, and he finally gave in. She promised to call him if anything changed.

Adam was exhausted and had decided to leave with Tom. He needed to get home and get some sleep. He promised he would be back the next day.

Autumn sighed and turned her attention to her mother. Leaning over, she whispered to her.

"Mama? It's Autumn. Jessie went to lie down for a while, and Dad is at home with Sam. Sam is fine, Mom. You don't have to worry about him. You just need to get better."

She paused a moment and then went on. "I need you to come back now, Mom. I want to talk to you about Adam, and the kids at school. Bre is bothering me now for some reason."

Autumn sat back and pushed her hair behind her ears. "Look, you can't leave me. I need you. You have to come back. I will take care of everything again. I'll do the dishes and take care of Sam and the house. You just need to come back."

There was no answer, no movement, no nothing. All Autumn could hear was the machine breathing for her mother. Tears filled her eyes as she looked at her.

"Mom," pleaded Autumn, her voice breaking. "Can you hear me? Talk to me. Yell at me. Say anything. Do something. Wake up. Look at me." She leaned in again. "Please," she whispered, tears running down her face. "Don't leave me here all alone."

The night nurse paused in the doorway, her heart breaking. It would take a miracle for Melissa to come out of the coma, and she didn't know if she believed in such things anymore. She straightened herself up and strode into the room, businesslike.

"You should be asleep," she told Autumn as she went over to check the machines buzzing and beeping in the room. "I've come to take vitals."

Autumn nodded and got up and walked over to the window. There was nothing to see outside but blackness. She didn't care. Everything she cared about was in this little room.

A whiff of lavender circled around her, reminding her of her mother's perfume. Autumn closed her eyes and breathed it in deeply as the nurse turned to speak to her.

"What are you doing?" asked the nurse, eyeing her.

"I smell lavender."

"Oh, that's probably my shampoo."

"My mother has a body spray she likes to wear that smells like that," murmured Autumn.

The nurse nodded. "I just wanted to let you know there seems to be a change in your mother's vitals. I'm going to have the doctor on call paged."

"What does that mean?" asked Autumn, fear in her eyes now.

The nurse saw this and tried to calm her. "The doctor should be here shortly. You can talk to him about it."

A grunt came from the bed, and Autumn and the nurse turned around to see Melissa reach up and attempt to pull out the breathing tube.

"Mom!" Autumn ran over to the bed to grab her mother's hand as the nurse tried to calm Melissa down. She pushed the button and asked for another nurse to come into the room.

"Go page the doctor," she instructed when another nurse arrived. The woman left quickly to do so.

"Mom, calm down. I know you don't like that thing in your throat, but it will be worse if you try to pull it out yourself," said Autumn anxiously. She was trying to hold back the tears in her eyes. "They went to get another nurse, so just hang on."

Noting the fear in her mother's eyes, she just kept on talking, hoping her babbling would distract her mother away from the breathing tube.

She sure hoped when the doctor came they would pull it out.

"Sam is alright. He is just a little scraped up," she said, sniffling a little and giving her mother's hand a squeeze. "Jessie is here, and Dad took Sam home earlier today. Do you want me to get Jessie? I can also call Dad . . ."

Another nurse and the doctor arrived, and Autumn was asked to leave the room. Thinking it was probably because of her age, she backed up and stood in the doorway. There was no way she was leaving.

They gathered around her mother, checking vitals and doing other things Autumn couldn't see. When they stepped away, the doctor shook his head.

"Everything looks okay for now," he said. "You seem to comprehend everything around you. Can you speak?"

It was then Autumn noticed the breathing tube was out and her mother was struggling to sit up. The nurse gently pushed her back down, telling her it was time for rest. Melissa shook her head.

"Tom," she managed to rasp out, and Autumn nodded.

"I'll go call him," Autumn said.

"Send respiratory therapy up here now. And send physical therapy up here tomorrow to do an assessment," directed the doctor. "She seems to be breathing on her own, but I want that monitored. I'm also concerned about her left arm. She's moving it clumsily; there may be some nerve damage there." He sighed and looked at Melissa's chart. "So I guess you need to call neurology up here as well."

He turned to give the nurse further instructions, adding, "Give her something to calm her down. I want her to rest."

"Melissa," he said, turning back around. "I am glad to see you back with us, but you are not out of the woods yet. I need you to calm down and relax. I'm going to send a boatload of people up here to check you out and make sure everything's in running order, alright? So close your eyes and rest until then."

He turned to glance at Autumn. "Your father should be called."

Autumn nodded.

"You and your family can come to see her, but only for a few minutes. She needs her rest. We're not out of the woods yet. Do you understand?"

"Yes," Autumn answered.

He nodded and then brushed past her and left. She tried not to run as she headed for the waiting room, where Jessie was asleep. She quickly woke her up, and they returned to the room together.

The nurses were moving about quietly and briskly while Melissa dozed. She moved agitatedly, and a few times one of the nurses reached over to pull the covers back up over her.

Jessie glanced at Melissa's pale face and shook her head. "Poor little thing," she said, shoving her hands in the front pockets of her blue jeans. "I wonder if the doctor would let me smudge her."

Autumn giggled in spite of herself. "You would probably set off the fire alarms."

Jessie grinned. "That's probably so."

"There are other things we can do," said Autumn.

"Yes, and we should go do them. Have you called your father?"

Autumn shook her head, and Jessie pulled out her phone. They walked back down the hall to the waiting room.

Jessie dialed her phone and talked briefly with her brother. Then she hung up and set it on the table.

"He still isn't happy with me being Melissa's medical advocate," said Jessie, sighing. "He is a proud man, and his mistakes keep getting thrown back into his face."

Autumn shook her head but said nothing, and after a moment, Jessie watched her look away.

"What is it?" she asked softly.

"It's nothing."

Nothing?"

"No. I'm fine."

Jessie stared at her a moment. "Is this about your father?"

"He doesn't deserve to be her medical advocate," she said sharply. "He left us."

"Have you still not forgiven your father for leaving your mom?"

"Nope."

"Why?"

"He hurt her. He hurt us."

"People make mistakes, even you," Jessie pointed out. "And he has apologized for them."

"Not to me. He needs to apologize to me for walking out on his family. He brought shame on this family. He made my life hard." Autumn got up and walked over to a chair across the room and sat down. "I don't want to talk about this anymore."

"Autumn . . ."

"No! I said I don't want to talk about it!" She crossed her arms and turned to face the wall to the left. "Let's just wait for Dad to show up. I'm tired. I want to go home."

"I have to go get him," replied Jessie, "and you need to come with me, I guess. You can be the one to watch Sam since you want to go home now."

"Fine with me."

"Autumn, you're acting like a child."

"Well, that's what everyone considers me anyhow."

"What has gotten into you? You were fine a few minutes ago."

"Mom's hurt and Dad's mad. Can you believe that? He leaves us and then wonders why he is not making decisions for Mom anymore. He has no right to do that." She shook her head. "Sam's hurt. School . . . well . . . sucks, frankly." She sighed. "I just want to close my eyes and make it all go away."

Jessie got up and walked over to the weary girl and pulled her head onto her shoulder. Autumn resisted for a moment and then wrapped her arms around her aunt and closed her eyes. She started to cry.

The Journal

A week later, Autumn's mother was in a rehabilitation center. Due to hitting her head on the pavement during the accident, she had several small strokes when she coded. One of them affected her swallowing, and she went into therapy for that. She was also having some trouble with balance, and she was working hard at her therapy so she could go home. She didn't like being confined.

Jessie's wedding plans were in full swing now. Melissa insisted that things go on as usual. She was helping with phone calls from her hospital bed and handled the invitation details. While Jessie was glad Melissa was feeling better, she didn't want her to overdo it. Melissa insisted the doctors wanted her to go on with her life as normally as possible. They said it would help her get well faster if she had something to look forward to.

Tom had been making daily trips to the hospital after work. He spent quiet evenings with Melissa and then went home after she fell asleep.

After he had walked into the waiting room and saw Jessie holding Autumn, who was crying, he hadn't been to the house much. Jessie told him Autumn was still upset with him for leaving them, and he didn't know what to do about it. On the one hand, it made him angry that she thought he should apologize to her. After all, it was Melissa who foisted all that work on her, not him. On the other hand, she wouldn't have done that if he hadn't left.

"There are two wolves inside each of us," Jessie had told him. "Each is filled with pride. One is good, the other is not. Which one will you feed?"

Autumn got up early one morning to braid her hair. She didn't do that often, but today she felt something in the air around her, so she grabbed her leather lacings and got to work. It was Wednesday, and her mother had been in rehab for a week and a half now.

No one was awake. Sam wouldn't be up for at least another hour, and Jessie would get him ready for day care before she left. She was going back to the city this morning.

As she brushed her long hair, Autumn thought about Adam. She hadn't seen a lot of him lately.

Her father had made her go back to school a few days ago, and now she was playing catch-up with her homework. She still had tutoring with Sydney, who was usually quiet most of the time. She was dealing with her own family issues, thought Autumn, tying a hair tie on the end of one braid.

There was a light knock at the front door and Autumn frowned, wondering who that could be. She walked down the hall and glanced at her mother's room, where Jessie was sleeping. There was no sound.

Autumn headed for the front door and pulled it open. There stood Adam.

"What are you doing here?" she asked.

"I thought we could walk to school together like we used to," he replied, eyeing her hair. "Um, is that a new hairstyle?"

"What? Oh . . ." Autumn touched her hair and then grinned. "You caught me in the middle of braiding. Come in while I finish."

She showed Adam to the couch and then headed back to her room again. She emerged a moment later with two braids in her hair with hair ties that matched her dress. She wore a pair of brown boots that brought out the brown in the flowers in her dress.

"You look nice," he said with a smile. "How's your mother doing?"

"Better," answered Autumn, grabbing her book bag. "She will probably be home in a week or two."

"That's good news," said Adam, getting up and heading for the door.

"I know." Autumn pulled open the front door and they went out.

Adam took her hand as they hit the pavement. He also took her books and balanced them with his own.

"Are you planning to do any more Jingle Dress dancing?"

Autumn shrugged. "I don't know at this point. Mom has to get better and come home. We won't know what she'll be left with after therapy." She sighed. "Things have pretty much gone back to the way they used to be."

"What do you mean?"

"Well, I am cooking and cleaning and taking care of Sam most of the time."

Adam frowned. "What about Jessie?"

"She is at rehab with Mom during the day. Then she picks Sam up and brings him home to me. She had to drop everything to come here when the accident happened. She had special order dream catchers to finish. They're done, so tomorrow she's leaving to go back to the city to drop them off. She's going to try to come back in a few weeks when Mom is released."

"Who will be picking Sam up from day care now?"

"Dad."

"I see. Has he moved back in?"

"Nope. I don't want him to, either."

"Why?"

"I'm still mad at him."

"Oh."

There was silence for a moment and then Adam stopped walking. Autumn stopped, too, surprised.

"What?" she asked.

"Are you going to tell me why you're mad at your dad or do I have to guess?"

Autumn shrugged.

"Okay . . . hmm . . . has he yelled at you and made your life miserable?"

Autumn shook her head.

"Has he ignored you?"

"No."

"Did he hurt Sam?"

"Of course not."

"So you're mad at him for no reason?"

Autumn started walking again. "Of course there's a reason."

"Which is?" Adam asked, jogging to catch up with her.

"He has a bad temper, called my mother a liar, and left the family, which made my life a mess."

"You mean that just happened?" Adam shook his head. "I would have never thought he would do that with your mom in rehab."

"No, he left before all this happened. You know that."

"Yes, I do." Adam put his arm around her as they headed across the yard to the school. "But I didn't know you still held a grudge against him. Hasn't he tried to make up for all that?"

Autumn shrugged and looked away.

"Hasn't your mother forgiven him?"

"Maybe, but I haven't."

"Why?"

"He hurt me."

"I know that. I'm sorry you had to go through it. Why can't you forgive him? Everyone makes mistakes. I think he's owned up to his. He certainly feels terrible about how things happened."

"I guess."

"How does hanging on to all this help?"

"I don't know how to let it go."

"Maybe you should talk to someone about it."

"I'm talking to you right now."

Adam smiled. "Yes, but I mean someone like a teacher or counselor."

"Dad doesn't like people in our business."

Adam opened the door to the school and walked in with Autumn. They were suddenly in a noisy, people-pushing hallway. Adam pulled Autumn closer and headed for her locker. Then they went to his.

The warning bell rang, and with one last smile, Adam headed down the hall to his first class of the day.

"Autumn?"

She turned around to see Sydney standing behind her.

"Miss Nottingham wants to see us right now," said Sydney, sighing. "She asked me to see if I could find you. Come on."

Autumn reluctantly trailed behind Sydney, pushing against all the students going in the opposite direction.

Sydney opened the door to the principal's office and then gestured for her to go in. Sydney shut the door behind them.

"We're here to see Miss Nottingham," said Sydney, and the secretary pointed to the open door to the principal's office. They went in.

"Hi, girls," said Miss Nottingham. "Sit down, please."

When the girls sat, she smiled at them.

"You're not in trouble. I just want to let you know that we have hired a new tutoring teacher, and you two will be working with her. Her name is Miss Carol. She asked me to give you these."

She handed the girls each a journal. Autumn's had a blue cover with an eagle on it, and Sydney had a red cover on hers.

"She would like you two to start journaling this week. Bring your journals along next week when you meet with her. You will see her every Tuesday at ten a.m."

"Um, Miss Nottingham," said Sydney, looking at the journal. "Someone could find this book and read it." She shook her head. "I don't want to do this."

"Yeah, writing is not my strong suit," added Autumn.

Miss Nottingham nodded. "No one is going to read it. It has a lock on it. Don't give anyone the key. There are two of them. One you will have, and one Miss Carol will have in case you lose yours."

She sighed and leaned forward. "Look, if you don't feel comfortable writing down your feelings, write down recipes, cartoons, sayings you like that you get off the internet. Just write three pages a week. Autumn, practicing writing the letters d and b will be helpful. Those have a tendency to be backward for you, right? And, Sydney, you could use some better skills with organizing your thoughts. At any rate, that's your homework from her. You may go now."

The girls left the office and headed down the hall. They had the same first class.

"This is stupid," muttered Sydney, fingering her journal.

Autumn said nothing. When they came to their classroom door, she pulled it open and they went inside.

"Where were you girls?" asked the teacher as they headed for their seats.

"At the principal's office," answered Sydney.

"Where's your hall pass?"

"She didn't give us one," replied Autumn, sitting down.

"How do I know you were there then?" asked the teacher frowning.

"Why would we make that up?" asked Sydney.

The teacher looked at the two of them for a moment and then went back to teaching the class.

Autumn slumped in her seat and opened her book.

"Autumn," said the teacher, "would you read the next paragraph for us, please?"

Autumn nodded and then swallowed hard. First the principal, and now this. Reading aloud was her least favorite thing to do.

She took a breath and, grimacing, started to read.

Starting Again

Melissa was anxious to go home. The doctor told her three more days, but she was getting restless and wanted to get back to her life.

The swallowing issue was getting better. She just needed to make sure she drank during her meals to keep her mouth moist. Her arm and hand were numb, but it was her left one and not her dominant one. She hated the feeling of it always being asleep, though. And strangely enough, it had shooting pain through it many times a day. For being numb, it sure was painful.

She knew how lucky she was, though. She could have died. Tom told her the young man who had hit her came to see her early on. She couldn't imagine why he would do that and wondered what she would say to him if he showed up again.

Melissa glanced at her watch, which she was now wearing on her other arm. It felt weird there, but she accepted things the way they were. Tom was running late, and she wondered if everything was alright at home.

A nice woman named Norma walked in with Melissa's supper.

"It's chicken tonight," Norma said cheerfully, and Melissa nodded.

After the woman left, Melissa pushed the tray table away and pushed herself up in the bed. She wanted to wait for Tom. They always ate together now, and she liked that. He usually brought in a burger and something special for her like ice cream or a donut. And she loved the lively discussions they had about everything from the kids to his work. She had missed that after he moved out, and she wondered what would happen when she was released and went home.

She sighed, lying back down. She turned on her side, facing the window, and closed her eyes to rest and wait for Tom.

She didn't hear him come in. He stood in the doorway with a bag of burgers in one hand and an ice cream sundae in the other.

Was she asleep? He stood there, unsure whether he should come in or not. He must have rustled the burger bag, because she turned over quickly and saw him.

"Tom! I didn't hear you come in." Melissa pulled herself up in the bed, and Tom walked in and set the burger bag down on the food tray.

"Is the ice cream for me?" she asked, smiling, and he nodded.

"I'll eat that first," she decided, popping the top off and digging in.

He grinned and sat down.

"You feeling okay?" he asked, and she nodded. Then she grimaced.

"Oh, wait."

He frowned. "What?"

"Brain freeze. Ate this too fast."

He laughed and watched as she made faces trying to warm up the ice cream in her mouth. After a moment she was digging back into the cup.

"So they plan to release you in a few days."

"Yes," she said, eyeing him. "Can you be my ride home?"

"I was planning on it."

"You don't have to work?"

"They know what's going on. I'll get the day off. I want to be sure you're settled in before I leave."

Melissa slowly set the ice cream down on the food tray Tom had moved back for her.

"What's the matter?" asked Tom, sitting forward. "Can I get you something?"

She shook her head and looked down at the blanket.

"What's the matter, Melissa?" Tom asked softly. He got up, and she moved over as he sat on the bed. He took her hand in his.

"Going home," she whispered. "Autumn will have to do almost everything again, and she has school. I don't want to put her in the position of having to do that again. It almost ruined our relationship."

Tom stared at her, and for a moment, neither spoke.

"How can I make this easier for you?" he asked, watching her.

She shrugged.

"You seem so unhappy. You should be glad to be going home."

"I am. It's just . . . overwhelming. I mean, I have the house to take care of, and Sam. I try to help Autumn with her homework and make supper. Work will be wondering when I will be returning."

"Don't rush that," he cautioned. "Wait until you're completely healed."

She nodded. "Yeah, but the rest of it won't wait."

"Autumn doesn't mind helping out."

"For a while. But she will probably start becoming resentful."

"She loves you, Melissa."

"I know."

"And so do I."

Melissa stared at him for a moment, taking in the warmth of his dark eyes.

"I love you, too," she said, and he smiled.

"Then let me come home."

"Hello," a man's voice interrupted.

The two of them turned to see the doctor walk in.

"Sorry, I'm running late," he said. "I haven't even had my dinner." He glanced down at the chart in his hand. "How are you today, Melissa?"

"Fine."

"Good to hear. It looks like you're going home soon."

She nodded, and he glanced up.

"Who will be there when you get home? You will be restricted for several weeks, and you may not return to work for a month yet."

"Restricted how?" she asked, frowning.

"No lifting over ten pounds, which basically means don't lift anything," he stated, glancing at the chart again. "You need to get plenty of rest and not jump back into everything right away. Slowly but surely is the best way to heal. Now, who will be at home with you after you have been released?"

"Well, my daughter is there."

"Does she have school?"

"Well, yes, but . . ."

"You can't be left alone for several weeks, Melissa. You are a fall risk."

"I'm sure I will be fine."

"And no driving for at least six weeks."

"I guess Sam stays home with me then," said Melissa, glancing at Tom. "I won't be working anyway, so I won't need day care."

"But you can't lift him," Tom pointed out, and the doctor nodded.

"Your arm and hand are not functioning properly," he said. "You have very little sensation in them. I don't know if that will get better. Whatever function you have after the first year is the best that it will be."

The doctor looked down at her chart again. "It might be possible to move you to a rest home for a while . . ."

"That won't be necessary," interrupted Tom. "I will be taking care of her myself."

The doctor looked over at him. "Pardon me, please, but I was under the impression you two were divorced."

"We are reconciling."

"I see." The doctor looked over at Melissa. "He will be there then?"

"I will work the second shift," said Tom. "By the time I leave, Autumn will be home. We will work in shifts."

"Well, fine then. It seems you have it all worked out. I will release you around ten in the morning on Friday. You will need to keep up with therapy until I see you in my regular office in a month. We'll go from there."

Tom watched the doctor leave and then turned to face Melissa. He would give a hundred dollars to know what she was thinking as she stared at him. Would she yell at him for taking over? Maybe she thought he was rearranging her life without any say from her. Not knowing what else to do, he held his breath and waited.

After what seemed like a lifetime of moments, Melissa spoke.

"Let's eat. I think the food's probably cold by now."

Tom smiled at her, and she smiled back. He grabbed the burger bag and sat down.

Nokomis

Autumn was sitting in tutoring class two weeks later, watching the teacher pull out a new assignment. She had been writing in her journal every day now. All her thoughts and feelings about Adam and her dad and the situation at home went in there, and somehow she felt better after writing them down. It was like she could let everything out without anyone criticizing or judging her about it.

"Sydney, have you been writing in your journal?" asked the teacher, eyeing her from across the room.

"Yes."

"Is there anything in there you would care to share?"

"Share?" Sydney shook her head. "I didn't know we were going to do that. That's private stuff."

"Yes, it is," agreed the teacher, walking over to the girls and sitting down at their table. "But sometimes it helps to get feedback on what we've written. It helps us see a different perspective."

"My perspective is just fine," Sydney replied. "I'll share."

The teacher and Sydney glanced over at Autumn in surprise.

She shrugged. "I could use some perspective on my life," she said, opening her book. She flipped through it for a moment and then settled on a page.

"This is from last week," she said. "Dad took Mom home from the hospital today," she read, "and he settled right in, as if he hadn't left. I came home from school to find him sitting on the couch with Mom. She was wrapped in my blanket. Why didn't she tell him that's the blanket Aunt Jessie made me? He must have gone in and took it right off my bed. I was mad when I saw it and went straight to my room. He has no right to walk in here like he owns the place when he clearly doesn't. I know they are trying to work it out, but no one asked me how I felt about him moving back in here."

Autumn stopped and closed the book. Sighing, she said, "I'm done."

"I'm sorry you are going through all that," said the teacher, reaching out to touch Autumn on the hand.

"Yeah."

Sydney didn't know what to say. She knew Autumn's parents were divorced and that her mom and Sam were in a terrible accident. Other than that, she hadn't given it much thought.

She looked over at Autumn, who sat quietly in the chair, fingering her journal. Autumn looked tired and worried, and for the first time, Sydney felt really bad for her. She thought back to all those times she had teased and tormented Autumn, and how Autumn hadn't really fought back. She had considered that weak, but she now realized it took strength not to fight back. Autumn could have lashed out with hurtful words back to her, but she didn't.

Sydney felt ashamed. But not enough to tell anyone that. Not just yet. She had her own problems with her parents. All that was in her journal. She picked it up and held it close to her chest, using it as a shield to protect herself. In here were her thoughts, and her words. They were for no one else to see or hear. Her journal was private.

The teacher glanced at her a moment and then said, "If Sydney doesn't want to read, we will move on. Here is a paragraph exercise I would like you to do. See if you can find the mistakes. Then fix the sentences the way they were supposed to be written."

Autumn went home that day knowing her dad wasn't going to be there. There ended up being an hour between the time he left for work and the time she got home. Usually her mom and Sam lay down during that time.

She was lonely. Adam couldn't walk her home. He was feeling under the weather and had stayed home from school.

Coming up the street to her house, Autumn noticed a car in the driveway. She didn't recognize it, but she thought maybe it was the physical therapist. She walked up the front pathway and went into the house. There at the dining room table sat her mother and an older lady. Sam was nowhere in sight. He must be napping, she thought.

"Autumn, come meet Mrs. Mengen."

Autumn dropped her book bag on the couch and walked over to them.

"I know who you are. You're Adam's nokomis."

The woman nodded.

"And you are the one Adam calls Miika."

Autumn blushed and looked at the floor. Her mother smiled and glanced at Mrs. Mengen, who was not smiling but watching Autumn intently.

"He doesn't bring you home to meet me," Mrs. Mengen said. "So, I come to you." She glanced at Melissa. "And to see if I can do anything for you," she added.

"Thank you," replied Melissa. "That was kind of you."

The old woman turned back to Autumn. "Please, sit down," she instructed. "I would like to talk to you."

Autumn did as she was told, and the women turned to face one another from across the table.

"Adam tells me you are going to a tutoring class for dyslexia," said Mrs. Mengen, and Autumn nodded.

"Yes, I am."

"How is that going?"

"Slow."

Mrs. Mengen nodded. "Good answer. Honest."

"She studies a lot at home," said Melissa, and Mrs. Mengen nodded.

"I'm sure she does," she replied.

Autumn sat in uncomfortable silence as the woman stared at her. Finally she said, "My grandson likes you very much."

Autumn nodded, embarrassed now.

"And what are your feelings for him?" she asked, watching Autumn closely.

"Oh, I don't think . . . ," said Melissa, but Mrs. Mengen put up a hand.

"I would like to hear it from her. I don't want my grandson getting hurt. If the feelings are one-sided, it's best he knows now."

"No."

The two women looked over at Autumn, who stared down at the table.

"I mean, no, they are not one-sided," she added.

Mrs. Mengen nodded.

"They are too young for any real feelings for each other," said Melissa, glancing at Autumn.

"The heart knows no age," said Mrs. Mengen. "You love who you love. Many people in the tribe have married young."

"Married? Oh, I don't think they are that committed to each other," said Melissa with a chuckle. "It's probably only puppy love at this point."

"Is that what it feels like, Autumn? Puppy love?" Mrs. Mengen shrugged. "Who's to say that won't grow into something more." She glanced over at Melissa. "I think your mother would like you to go slow, however."

Autumn nodded, hoping the woman would move on to another topic. This one was embarrassing.

"Um, I have some homework to do," Autumn said, getting up from the table.

"Alright," said Melissa, glancing over at Mrs. Mengen. "If you don't mind, I think we should cut this visit short. I usually nap at this time, while Sam is down for his."

"Of course."

The woman got up and headed for the door. Autumn went over to grab her book bag off the couch as the woman turned around to stare at her one more time.

"Miika," she murmured, "My grandson is right. Kind in your heart, too. He has made a good choice."

Autumn and her mom watched as the woman opened the door and left, pulling it shut behind her. Melissa turned to Autumn.

"Wow, that was intense."

"Yeah," Autumn said.

"So, do you really have homework, or were you trying to get away?" Melissa smiled, and Autumn laughed.

"A little of both," she admitted.

"Listen, before you go, I want to ask you something."

Autumn lifted her school bag off the couch and waited.

"Are you okay with Dad moving back in here? You hardly speak to him and spend a lot of time in your room."

"I'm a teenager, Mom," Autumn answered evasively, slinging the bag over her shoulder. "We spend a lot of time in our room."

"So everything's okay with Dad?"

Autumn sighed, and started for her room.

"Everything's fine, Mom."

"Autumn, stop, please."

Autumn stopped but didn't turn around. "What?"

"You've been upset since I came home." Melissa stopped and looked away. "Is it me? Have I done something?"

Autumn turned around to see sadness in her mother's eyes.

"No. Don't think that." She shook her head.

"Then it is Dad?"

Autumn shrugged.

"Why? Don't you want him here?"

"I don't think he's earned the right to move back in here after all he's done."

"Everyone makes mistakes," Melissa said.

"He didn't seem too sorry about them."

"He is trying to make it up to me."

"But not to me," said Autumn.

"You?"

"Yes, me!"

"Why would he have to do that?"

"Are you kidding?" Autumn dropped her book bag on the floor and took a step toward her mother.

"He yelled at you and called you names. Then he left us without a look back. You went crazy, and I had to pick up the slack and do everything around here. We almost didn't get through that, Mom. Look what happened to us. I ran away, remember?" She turned back around and picked up her book bag. "I hate him for that, Mom. He doesn't deserve a second chance."

"What happened to make you so hard?" asked Melissa. "No one is perfect. We all make mistakes, and if we see them, we try to do better."

"He doesn't understand what he did to us, Mom."

"Yes, he does. I talked to him."

"Yes, but he hasn't talked to me about them. Not really. I mean, we have talked, and I love him, Mom. He's my dad, you know. On the one hand, I want him here. I want us to be a family again. But he should apologize to me for what he put me through. Sam's too young to remember all this, but I am not."

She turned to go. "Until he does that, I have no use for him. His actions have affected everything in my life. Even my relationship with Adam."

"That's a choice you're making. It doesn't have to be that way."

Autumn turned to stare at her, and Melissa teared up with the pain she saw in her daughter's eyes.

"Kids learn what they see, Mom," Autumn whispered. "And I've seen too much to think life is full of roses and beautiful music." She shook her head. "Mrs. Mengen doesn't have to worry. There's not much hope for Adam and me. If I've learned anything, it's that no matter what you do, relationships don't work."

Tears slipped down Melissa's face as she watched her daughter go down the hall and into her room. The door clicked when her daughter shut it, effectively shutting her out, too.

CHAPTER

9

The Healing Begins

A few days later, Autumn was sitting in class, when her father arrived. It was after a lunch she didn't bother to try to eat, and now she was doodling an abstract picture on her notebook cover.

"Autumn, can you come up here, please?" asked her teacher, motioning her to come to her desk.

Autumn frowned, but got up and moved slowly toward the front of the room. The teacher told her she was wanted in the office, so she went back and gathered her things and headed there.

As she walked down the hall, she wondered what was wrong now. Her life seemed to go from bad to worse, and she didn't know how much more she could take at this point.

She came to the office door and pushed it open to find her father sitting in a chair next to the secretary's empty desk.

They stared at each other for a moment and then he stood.

"Come on; let's go."

Autumn didn't say a word, but followed him out the door. She wondered for a moment if Adam would be curious about where she went when he would try to walk her home after school. She sighed and then shrugged, shifting her books to her other arm. He would find her already gone, and that was that.

They made a stop at her locker and then headed out to the parking lot. Tom opened the door for her, and she reached in to throw her bag in the back of the truck. Then she turned to glance at him.

"Is there something wrong with Mom?" she asked, and her father shook his head.

"Sam's alright?"

He nodded. "Get in."

She watched him walk around the truck and slide in, and she followed suit.

"Where are we going?"

"Someplace where we can talk," he said, and she shook her head.

"I don't want to talk. I don't have anything to say."

He nodded. "Good. Then you can listen, because I have plenty to say."

He never took his eyes off the road, and she sat back, frowning. The last thing she needed was him yelling at her.

They pulled into a family friend's driveway, and Autumn turned to look at her father.

"What are we doing here?" she asked. "Is Ed here now? I thought he had gone to his daughter's house in the Twin Cities."

"He has," replied her father. "He said I could come here if I wanted to fish the shoreline. Today I want to walk it."

Her father got out and started walking toward the water. Autumn watched him a moment and then slowly got out of the truck. She wasn't sure what was expected of her, and her father was acting very strange at the moment. She stayed by the truck until her father noticed and gestured her out to the shore. When she stopped in front of him, he gestured for her to walk with him.

"When I was a boy, my father used to beat the crap out of me," he said. Startled, Autumn turned to look at him.

"I didn't know that," she muttered, and he nodded.

"No one does, not even your mother. I think that's why I have a lot of anger in me."

"In the last year, I have had to tame that side of me, that dark wolf who rears his head now and again." Her father bent down to pick up a smooth, flat stone and threw it across the water, making skipping sounds.

"My mother used to call that 'skipping stones,'" he added, watching the stone skim across the water. "Have you tried it?"

Autumn nodded and searched the shore for a good skipper stone. When she found one, she expertly skipped it several times across the water.

Her father nodded in approval. "Good job." He turned to look at her. "You and I are a lot alike."

Autumn shrugged and resumed walking, and her father watched her for a moment. Then he started walking behind her.

"We both have too much pride," he added, watching her, but she still didn't stop walking or turn around.

He caught up to her and gestured for her to sit down in the sand. She sighed and then sat. He dropped down next to her.

"You're mad at me, is that right?"

When she didn't respond, he turned to stare at the water.

"I understand why you come to the water for calming," he said. "This is aun-way-be-win for you."

She nodded. "Yes, this is a resting place for me. But lately, I have not found any rest anywhere."

"You have a cluttered mind," he said, picking up a little pebble and palming it in his hand. It was jagged on one side, and he held it up to her.

"You are like this pebble," he said, "jagged on one side and smooth on the other."

Autumn's eyes narrowed and she looked away, not understanding.

"Autumn, the things that happen to us, the choices we make, shape who we are," he said. "Some of us turn out misshapen; some have pieces missing; and others become smooth and round."

She turned to look at him now.

He shook his head. "I made a lot of mistakes in my life before your mother came along, and I have made terrible ones since she's been in my life. But I have no regrets. Each bad choice was a lesson that taught me something."

"You don't regret leaving Mom? What that did to us?" Autumn sneered and turned away. "I told Mom you weren't sorry."

"Oh, that's where you are wrong. I am very sorry."

"But you just said . . ."

"I said I have no regrets because I learned something."

"Regret, sorry . . . same thing."

"No, they aren't."

Autumn turned back toward her father and saw him staring out across the water now.

"The water laps against the shore all day," he said, "and in its wake, it sometimes destroys things, washes sand over the little holes made by bugs and creatures that live here. It covers up their houses and places to hide, washing them away so they have to rebuild time and again."

He turned to look at her. "If it could, it might be sorry for doing that to those things that are affected by its movement, but it has no regrets. It is in the water's nature to lap against the shore day after day."

He reached out and took her hand. "It is our nature to make mistakes in this life. If we regret them, then we couldn't learn from them. But we can be sorry to have hurt someone else during our learning process."

Autumn looked into his eyes and saw him staring back. "I am so sorry I hurt you," he said quietly. "My heart hurts for the pain I caused you and your mother and Sam. I let the pain I have been carrying around in my heart affect those I love, and I lost everything good I ever had. All I can do now is hope that you will be patient with me as I learn and grow from the pain my actions have caused." He paused and then added, "I guess I am asking for grace."

"What do you mean?" she whispered. "What's grace?"

"It's when you forgive someone who doesn't deserve it."

Autumn stared into her father's eyes. They were the same dark brown as hers and had the same tears in them as hers did.

"I'm sorry, too," she said, bowing her head in shame. "I hurt those around me, too. I was mean to Mom and Adam, and you. I was afraid . . ."

"I know, sweetheart." He reached out and pulled her into his arms while she cried. "Everything's going to be alright now."

As the wind picked up over the water, the lapping waves started rushing toward them. Tom pulled away and smiled down at his daughter.

"Let's go home," he said with a smile, and she nodded.

Hand in hand, they walked back to the car.

Coming to Understand

Sydney watched Autumn walk into school
without Adam the next day. She wondered
what happened to him and why he wasn't there.
Did they break up?

Autumn didn't see Sydney as she made her
way down the hall and to her locker. She was
preoccupied with the large project due in that day,
and she knew she had to give her presentation
first. She was very nervous and wished Adam
wasn't sick. He was always a great confidence
booster for her.

Sighing, she stopped by her locker and tried
the lock, which, of course, she couldn't get open
the first time.

"Here, let me," someone said, and Autumn
looked up to see Sydney standing there.

"What?"

Sydney shrugged. "Let me try. Sometimes they
stick."

Autumn stepped back, and Sydney swirled the lock around and back again. On the third number, the lock dropped open and Sydney smiled.

"There you go."

"How did you know my locker combination?" asked Autumn with a frown.

Sydney smiled. "I peeked once when we were talking a while back."

Talking . . . well, that wasn't the correct term for being harassed, but Autumn didn't say so.

She jammed her stuff on the top shelf and dragged out everything she needed for the presentation. Sydney eyed the rolled-up poster.

"Who's your project on?"

"Christopher Columbus."

Sydney laughed. "Really? What rotten luck to get him."

"Yeah, I know," smiled Autumn. "There's absolutely nothing exciting about him. I had to really dig to get something interesting to say about him."

"I bet."

There was an awkward silence for a moment and then Autumn spoke up.

"Why are you being so nice to me? You hate me."

Sydney shook her head, "I don't hate you. You are just fun to tease. Making fun of people is my hobby."

"I think you need a different hobby."

Sydney nodded. "Yeah, I was thinking that, too." She glanced over Autumn's shoulder to see Jayden and Bre heading their way. "Maybe I should find some new friends, too."

Autumn turned around and groaned. They were heading straight for her and she would be surrounded. She looked back to see Sydney shaking her head.

"Don't leave," she said quietly. "I started this, and now I'll handle the situation."

"No," replied Autumn, backing away. "You don't have to."

"So, Sydney, I see you found our good friend, Autumn," said Bre. "We were just looking for her."

"Why?" replied Sydney, glancing from Bre to Jayden.

"We just want to talk to her," answered Jayden, grinning now.

Autumn went to speak, but Sydney put up her hand. Autumn stayed silent.

"We were just leaving for class," said Sydney. "Maybe later."

The girls' eyes opened wide and then narrowed at the look on Sydney's face.

"You're sticking up for her now?" asked Jayden.

"Yeah, what does she have on you?" asked Bre.

"Excuse me? What is that supposed to mean, Bre?" asked Sydney, glaring at her.

"Well, you have become awfully chummy with someone you used to harass all the time," answered Jayden. "There has to be a reason."

"There is a reason."

"Which is?"

"I grew up, Jayden. I suggest you do the same."

The girls laughed.

"Whatever," replied Jayden, flipping her hair over her shoulder.

"You grew up. Really?" asked Bre, laughing now.

"Come on, Autumn," said Sydney. "There's no one worth talking to here."

Autumn reluctantly followed Sydney to class as the two girls sputtered indignantly behind them. She heard a lot of "Who does she think she is, talking to us like that?" and "What happened to her? She is such a . . ."

"Autumn, ignore them," instructed Sydney. "They're clueless."

"Why did you do that?"

Sydney stopped in the doorway of the classroom and sighed.

"I don't know. I guess I'm tired of being someone no one likes. I mean, I have friends, but not the right kind." She shook her head. "My life sucks, and I guess I took that out on a lot of people." She stopped and caught Autumn's eye. "Including you."

Autumn waited, but nothing more came from Sydney. It was as close to an apology as she was ever going to get, so she smiled and nodded and then moved into the room to sit down. Sydney gave her a little smile and sat down on the other side of the room. Autumn knew they weren't best friends, but they seemed to have come to some kind of understanding.

A half hour later, Autumn stood up and gave her presentation. She stuttered a little in the beginning, but overall the teacher said she did well. She sat down with a renewed sense of confidence and relief.

Just before the bell rang signifying the end of the class, someone came from the front office to talk to the teacher. They glanced at Sydney and then gestured to her. Sydney walked up to the teacher and listened as she was told that her mother was there to pick her up.

Frowning, Sydney went back to her desk and gathered her stuff. Then she headed out of the room, passing by Autumn's desk. Autumn gave her a reassuring smile, and Sydney nodded.

It wasn't until the end of the day that Autumn discovered that Sydney was moving. She was to finish out the week, and then they were moving over the weekend. It was a shock to everyone, including Autumn, who now wondered how this would affect the situation with Bre and Jayden. She almost wished that she was moving, too, but then she thought of Adam and smiled, knowing she would be heartbroken to move away from him.

Hmm . . . that was an interesting thought. Autumn walked home later, pondering that. If she would be heartbroken to be away from him, then she must really like him a lot. It was the first time she really admitted that to herself, and it scared her a little. If her feelings were that deep, then he had the ability to hurt her. She didn't want that. Maybe she should break up with him before he broke up with her. That would hurt less, right? Or maybe not. Autumn bit her lip, thinking.

She sighed. She wished Aunt Jessie was here. Maybe she could call her. Autumn smiled and walked a little faster.

She would go home and call her. Aunt Jessie would know what to do.

A Clear Mind

essie was at the bridal salon picking out a veil when Autumn called.

"Hang on a minute, honey," she said, setting the veil down. The saleswoman gave her some privacy as Jessie sat down on a soft-cushioned gold couch.

"Okay, I'm back," said Jessie. "Oh, I'm at the bridal salon again. No, I haven't changed my mind about the dress. I'm picking out a veil. Yes, I know I wasn't going to wear one, but Ryan wanted me to." Jessie smiled. "It seems I'm doing a lot of things for him these days."

Jessie listened as Autumn turned the conversation toward what's been happening at home and the talk she had with her dad at the lake. Then she spoke about Sydney moving and how the girl almost apologized to Autumn. Jessie listened patiently for a while, and when Autumn took a breath, she jumped in.

"So, it's been pretty hectic over there," she said. "I'm glad things seem to be working out for your family."

"Yeah," replied Autumn. "It looks like things might be okay in the end."

"Honey, I appreciate the update, but I am at the bridal salon . . ."

Autumn sighed and then sat down on the bed.

"I know. I just wanted to talk to you about something."

"There's more?"

"Yeah." Autumn sighed and kicked off her shoes. She had called Jessie the second she had gotten home. Everyone was napping, and Autumn was alone in her room.

"What is it?"

"I wanted to talk to you about Adam."

"He hasn't been pressuring you to do things, has he? You know what I mean. Because if he is . . ."

"No, nothing like that. He wouldn't do that," replied Autumn, pushing her hair behind her ears. "Look, I think I might break up with him."

"Why on earth would you do that? Has he done something?"

Autumn shook her head. "No, nothing like that."

"Okay, I'm confused then," said Jessie.

"I just don't think it's going to work out. I called because I thought you might have some idea on how to go about doing this without hurting him."

"No, there is no way to go about doing this without hurting him."

"Oh."

"Autumn, don't you like him anymore?"

"I like him."

"You do?"

"Yes. I like him a lot."

"So, to show him how much you like him, you're going to break up with him?"

Autumn laughed. "I guess it sounds dumb when you put it that way."

"Well, yeah!"

Autumn didn't speak for a moment and Jessie frowned.

"What is it? What's going on?"

"I don't know," replied Autumn. "I guess I'm afraid."

"Of what?"

Autumn took a deep breath and the words came tumbling out.

"I think I like him too much and maybe he doesn't like me that way and then if I let myself get too involved with him he will hurt me." She bit her lip. "Or I'll scare him off . . . or something like that." She hesitated, and then added, "And my family is a handful. I mean, Dad is Dad, and . . ."

"This all sounds like fear of getting hurt. Don't you feel like you deserve to be happy?"

"I don't know. I said I was afraid." She sighed. "I don't have much to offer him . . ."

"You are a wonderful girl and deserve to have some happiness in your life, Autumn. You are enough for someone."

Autumn teared up and sniffled as Jessie went on.

"It's okay to be afraid," said Jessie. "It means you're putting yourself out there and not taking him for granted. That's a good thing."

"None of this feels like a good thing," said Autumn. "All I do is worry."

"I don't understand that. It's so obvious how much he likes you, even when you pull away from him."

"I don't do that . . ."

"Yes, you do," interrupted Jessie. "And it hurts him. Even your father noticed."

"What? When did he see me pulling away from Adam?"

"In the car on the way home from the pow wow."

"Oh." She sighed. "Look, Aunt Jessie, I don't know if it's such a good idea to have a relationship with anyone right now. My family life is a mess, and I am still trying to work through my dyslexia issues."

"This all sounds like excuses. Love doesn't always come at the perfect time," said Jessie. "And relationships are hard work. No one's is perfect. There's a lot of give and take. If you're not willing to do that, then maybe you should let him go."

"That's what I'm saying."

"I'm not so sure that's what you're saying at all. I think you're saying you don't want to put in the time to make the relationship with Adam work."

"What? That's not what I'm saying at all! Why would you think that?" Autumn shook her head angrily. "Aren't you listening to me?"

"Yes, I am. But you're making no sense."

"Yes, I am." Autumn sighed. "Maybe calling you was not such a good idea."

"Why? Because you are afraid you will hear the truth? Well, I've always told you the truth, and I'm not going to mince words with you now. You're scared your relationship will turn out like your parents', so you are pushing Adam away. This way, you don't get hurt. Never mind that this boy has been with you through thick and thin. Oh, I'm not saying you should run off and marry him or that you're even in love with him.

I'm just saying you need to treat him with the same respect he's treated you."

"I have always . . ."

"No, you haven't," said Jessie, interrupting her now. "You blow hot and cold all the time. I bet he doesn't know where he stands with you right now."

When Autumn went silent, Jessie sighed. "Look, honey. If you don't like him the way he likes you, then let him go so he can move on with his life without you. But don't let fear take things away from you."

"I don't know what I feel."

"That's an honest answer. So let me ask you this then. If he were to move away and you would never see him again, how would you feel? Would you wish him well and move on with your life or would you miss him terribly? When you can answer that question, you will know how you feel."

"I would miss him," whispered Autumn. "I would miss him a lot." She started to tear up just thinking about him going away.

"Then go slow," said Jessie softly. "There's no hurry. You guys are young and have plenty of time. Maybe you'll end up together or maybe not. If it ends, make sure you have no regrets, okay? 'Cause you have to live with those."

Autumn was quiet for a moment, and Jessie smiled.

"I guess you're growing up, young lady. Man, you have come so far in the last year. You were shy and unsure when I first got to know you, and now you have confronted your dyslexia and family troubles head on. I am so proud to call you my niece."

Autumn teared up and smiled.

"Thanks," she said, with a knot stuck in her throat. "It helps having someone to talk to."

"You have your parents," Jessie pointed out, and Autumn smiled and shook her head.

"Who do I talk to when they're the problem?"

Jessie laughed. "Me, I guess."

"Yeah. Thanks, Aunt Jessie."

"Of course. I love you, Miika."

"Hey, Adam calls me that."

"Ryan calls me that," replied Jessie, and Autumn smiled.

"I guess that's why you're marrying him."

"Well, one of the reasons."

"Talk to you later," said Autumn, and Jessie nodded.

"Yup. Call me again if you need straightening out."

"Hey!" Autumn laughed. "Talk to you later."

"Bye, Autumn."

Autumn heard a click and her aunt was gone. She set the phone down on her bed and leaned back. Things were clearer now in her mind. She knew what she needed to do and wanted to get started right away.

But there was no hurry. She closed her eyes and smiled. She had all the time in the world. There would be plenty of time for her life to unfold.

The conversation with Aunt Jessie was exhausting, and she was tired. Yawning, she snuggled down into her covers and smiled as she drifted off to sleep.

CHAPTER 1

The Medicine Wheel

Autumn was working on her typing skills in tutoring class. If she could just remember where all the letters on the keyboard were, she wouldn't have to look at the keyboard to try to pick them out. She saw some of the letters backward, and this was a constant source of frustration for her.

"Good, Autumn," praised the teacher, glancing over her shoulder at her work. "Only one mistake. Here, take a look. This letter is next to the one you were looking for."

Autumn stared down at the laptop and nodded. It did look pretty good. She smiled.

"You know, there are plenty of jobs where computer skills are needed," said her teacher. "Have you given any thought to what you want to do after high school?"

Autumn shook her head. "I never thought I would get past high school," she admitted. "I never thought college was an option for me."

"I think you would do well in college," replied the teacher. "You're smart and have a lot of things going for you. There is financial aid to help you as well."

When Autumn didn't respond, the teacher nodded. "Well, you think about it, okay? You have some time to make that decision."

A little while later, Autumn sat down across from Sydney. During the last half of the tutoring class, they would be discussing their journaling.

This was Sydney's last day at school, as she was moving that weekend. Autumn didn't know how she felt about it. The girl wasn't bothering her anymore, but they weren't friends, either. They seemed to have come to some sort of understanding between them, but Autumn wasn't sure what that was.

"I would like to read today," said Sydney, and the teacher smiled.

"I was hoping you would do that," she replied.

Sydney opened her book and stared down for a minute.

"Dad showed up last night. Mom let him in, and they started to argue right away," she read. "When Mom asked him to leave, he wouldn't go."

Sydney stopped there a moment, glancing up at Autumn. Then she looked back down at her book.

"When I walked into the room, Dad told me to get my stuff, we were leaving. I told him no, I was going with Mom. He got even madder after that, and it was all Mom could do to push him out the door and lock it behind him. He kept pounding on the door until Mom told him she would call the police if he didn't leave. A few minutes later, we could hear a siren in the distance and the pounding stopped. Mom didn't call anybody, but Dad didn't know that. He left right away. The police just passed by before heading someplace else."

Sydney closed the book. "My uncle is staying with us until we move. Mom called him this morning. I guess she thought we weren't safe anymore."

The teacher patted Sydney's hand. "I'm sorry you're going through all that," she said quietly. "I wish only the best for you and your family."

Sydney nodded and then glanced at Autumn.

"I thought maybe you would understand," she said.

Autumn nodded.

"I mean, with your dad and all . . ."

Sydney trailed off and looked away, and Autumn nodded again.

"I understand," she said.

"I hear your dad has moved back in," said Sydney.

"Yes."

"How it that going? I mean, is he still . . ."

"No," interrupted Autumn. "He is better now."

"I see." Sydney paused, and then added, "I don't see things getting better between my mom and dad."

"I'm sorry."

"Yeah, me, too."

The bell rang and Autumn and Sydney left the classroom and walked down the hall together. They both noted how everyone around them watched them with curiosity. Sydney grinned.

"We are making a scene," she said, moving her books to the other arm.

Autumn nodded.

"I guess I must have given you a hard time."

"Yes."

They came to Sydney's next class. She paused, but Autumn didn't.

"Autumn?"

Autumn stopped and turned slightly, not meeting Sydney's eyes.

"Thanks," she said, and Autumn frowned.

"For what?"

Sydney shrugged. "Listening."

"You're welcome."

"Bye."

"Goodbye."

Autumn watched Sydney disappear into the classroom, and then she turned around and started walking to her own. She probably wouldn't see Sydney again, but she was okay with that. They'd said all they needed to.

After school she walked by Adam's house. She hadn't seen him in a while, since he had been sick enough to stay home for several days. She looked wistfully into the living room window, hoping to catch a glimpse of him.

"Who are you looking for?"

She whipped around to see Adam standing behind her. He had been sitting on his front doorstep, hoping to see her leave school for the day. When she passed by his house into his backyard, he got up and followed her.

"I was . . . you. I was looking for you," she admitted, laughing, and he smiled.

"Well, here I am."

"I see that. How are you doing?"

"Alright. Did you miss me?"

"Yes."

He grinned and pulled her to him. He gave her a kiss on the forehead, and when she frowned, he laughed.

"I am just getting over being sick," he said. "I don't want to kiss you on the mouth until I am sure I'm better."

"Oh."

"Can I walk you home?"

"Are you sure it's alright?"

"Yes."

"Alright then."

They headed down the street, hand in hand.

"I washed my hands before coming outside," he said, noting Autumn's glance down at them, and Autumn nodded.

"Good idea."

"So, what's been happening?"

"Well, you know Sydney's last day is today."

"Yeah, I heard that. Are you glad she's leaving?"

"I don't know."

Adam frowned. "Really? After everything she's put you through?"

"Yeah. She was mean, but I guess I understand. Her home life was not the best."

"That's no reason to take it out on others."

Autumn nodded. "I think she realizes that now."

"Did you two talk?"

"Sort of."

"And?"

"And I'm okay with it all now."

Adam frowned. "I'm not sure I understand, but that's alright. As long as you're happy."

"I am," she said. "Now I want to talk about something else. That's why I came looking for you today."

Adam was silent a moment, glancing into her face. He gripped her hand harder.

"Everything's okay, right? With us, I mean. You're not having second thoughts again? I know I haven't been around much, but . . ."

"No, everything's fine, but I did want to talk about us."

"I see. Okay, what's wrong?"

"Adam, nothing is wrong. Geez, do I make you that insecure?"

"Well, you blow hot and cold all the time, and I never know . . ."

"Yes, I know."

"You do?"

Autumn nodded. "Yes, that was pointed out to me earlier."

"Who said something?"

"Never mind. Anyway, I just wanted you to know I made up my mind about us."

"And?"

Autumn went silent for a moment, knowing she had to choose her words carefully. She wanted everything to come out right. This was so important . . .

"Autumn, you're killing me!" said Adam, interrupting her thoughts. He stopped and turned to look at her. "Tell me," he pleaded.

"I want to be your girlfriend," she said, and then smiled. "If you want that, too, I mean."

Adam hugged the life out of her and then kissed her on the mouth anyway, despite his good intentions.

"I've thought of you that way ever since I met you," he said. "But I've been so afraid of being dumped. You seem to like me one minute, and then the next minute you push me away." He frowned. "I didn't know what to think."

"Your getting sick was probably the best thing that could have happened," she said.

He shoved his hands in his front jean pockets and shook his head. "I don't understand. How did that affect anything?"

"I didn't see you for a while. It gave me time to think and made me realize how much I missed you," she replied, and he smiled.

"I'm glad I got sick, then."

Autumn laughed and then took his hand as they started walking toward her house.

"Do you think your dad will let me start dating you on a regular basis?" he asked. "I know we went out a couple of times, but he moved back in with your family and things might be different now." He shrugged. "I don't know how he feels about things."

"I will talk to him about it," she said. "I want that, too. By the way, I got my invitation to Aunt Jessie's wedding. They sent them out early. Will you be my date?"

He frowned. "Well, who else would you go with? I'm your boyfriend."

She laughed and nodded. "I guess that's so."

"Besides," he added, "I got my own invitation."

"She sent you one? That's awesome!"

"I know. I was excited to get it. I really want to go. I like your aunt very much."

"She likes you, too."

"Since you're wearing a long formal dress, I thought I would wear my suit," he said with a smile.

"You'll look great in it."

"I hope so. I was also thinking about cutting my hair."

Autumn stopped dead. "What? You'll do no such thing! Why on earth would you want to do that?"

He shrugged. "Well, it's really long, and I thought if I cut it I would look more grown-up and . . ."

"Nope. You are not to cut your hair. I like it long."

"But . . ."

"No!" she interrupted firmly. "You don't need to look any more grown-up than you do now. I don't want every girl in school giving you the come-hither look."

"The come-hither look?" Adam laughed so hard, he started coughing. "Sorry about that," he said, trying to catch his breath. "I still have this cough, and . . ."

"There's nothing funny about what I said," replied Autumn, eyeing him. "You're my boyfriend, and I get a say in what you do with your hair. I like it long."

"My gosh, you have gotten so bossy," replied Adam, with a grin. "Alright then, I won't cut my hair." He picked up her hand and they started walking again. "But you will not always have a say in things like that," he warned.

"We'll see," she replied, and he laughed again.

"Race you to the house," he challenged, and she frowned.

"You are still sick. Running is not good for someone with a cough."

"I will decide that," he stated, eyeing her. "So, if I beat you to your front door, I get to pick where we go on our next date. If you win, you get to decide. Deal?"

Autumn grinned and then shot out ahead of him.

"It's a deal," she yelled over her shoulder, and he took off after her.

"You cheated," he said, coming up fast behind her.

She laughed as they entered her driveway.

He reached out to grab her before she could get to the front door and swung her around, effectively putting her behind him. Then he reached out to touch the door.

"I win," he said, gasping for air. He coughed a few times and then started to laugh at the expression on her face.

"You cheated!" she said, grabbing his arm.

"So did you," he pointed out, and then pulled her to him, kissing her again.

Pushing him away, she grabbed his hand and pulled him down on the front step to sit next to her. She dropped her head on his shoulder and he smiled, bending toward her.

As they laughed and talked, Melissa watched them from the living room window. Her daughter was happy, and that was all that mattered to her. Tom may not be excited about his daughter's budding relationship, but he would have to get over it. Autumn was growing up, whether they liked it or not.

Adam was part of Autumn's Medicine Wheel of life. Tom had taught her that every part of the wheel is important and reliant on the other parts. One thing affects another, and the wheel is not complete without all the parts.

It was apparent that Adam was a part of Autumn's Medicine Wheel because he brought her harmony, balance, and respect.

Melissa turned away from the window and smiled. That was all any parent could ask for.

NEUHAUS ACADEMY

neuhausacademy.org

Neuhaus Academy helps teenage and adult learners improve their reading, spelling, and comprehension skills through simple online instruction. All lessons are individually tailored to each person's specific needs so that learners can work at their own pace. The courses are always free for learners and can be customized by instructors to promote and ensure a successful outcome.

FRIENDS OF QUINN

friendsofquinn.com/for-young-adults

Friends of Quinn is an online community that connects and inspires people affected by learning differences. It offers resources, social networking, and support for young adults with learning differences and for the people who love them. The website was founded by Quinn Bradlee, filmmaker and author of *A Different Life,* a book about growing up with learning differences.

SMART KIDS WITH LEARNING DISABILITIES

smartkidswithld.org

Smart Kids with Learning Disabilities aims to educate, guide, and inspire parents of children with learning disabilities or ADHD. Its goal is to help parents realize their children's significant gifts and talents and to show that with love, guidance, and the right support, their children can live happy and productive lives.

UNDERSTOOD

for learning & attention issues

understood.org

The mission of Understood is to support the millions of parents whose children are struggling with learning and attention issues. The organization strives to empower parents and help them better understand their children's issues and experiences. With this knowledge, parents can then make effective choices that propel their children from simply coping to truly thriving.

CHILD MIND INSTITUTE

childmind.org

The Child Mind Institute is an independent national nonprofit dedicated to transforming the lives of children and families struggling with mental health and learning disorders. Its objectives are to deliver the highest standards of care, advance the science of the developing brain, and empower parents, professionals, and policymakers to support children whenever and wherever they need it most.

ABOUT THE AUTHOR

KIM SIGAFUS is an award-winning Ojibwa writer and Illinois Humanities Road Scholar speaker. She has coauthored two 7th Generation books in the Native Trailblazers series of biographies, including *Native Elders: Sharing Their Wisdom* and the award-winning *Native Writers: Voices of Power*. Her fiction work includes the PathFinders novels *Nowhere to Hide* and *Autumn's Dawn*, which are the first two books in the Autumn Dawn series, and The Mida, an eight-volume series about a mystically powerful time-traveling carnival owned by an Ojibwa woman. Kim's family is from the White Earth Indian Reservation in northern Minnesota. She resides with her husband in Freeport, Illinois. For more information, visit kimberlysigafus.com.